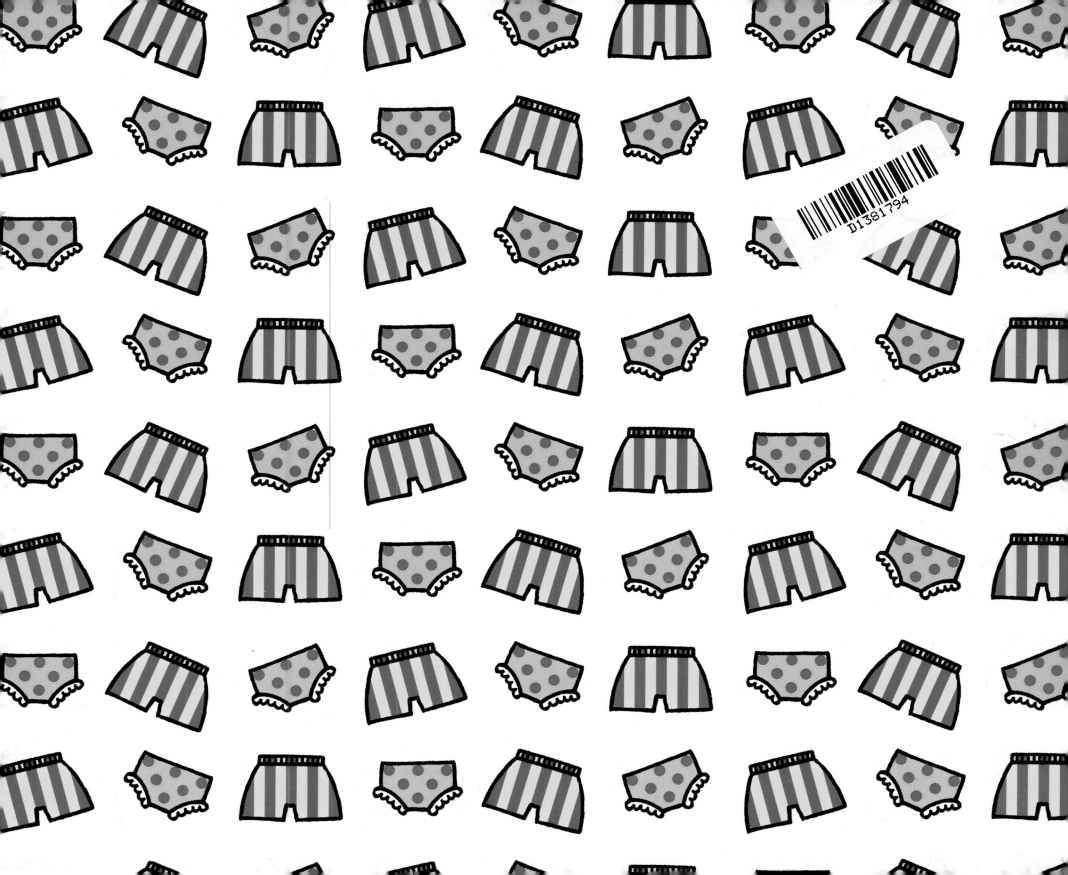

PUFFIN BOOKS

UK | USA | Canada | Ireland | Australia
India | New Zealand | South Africa

Puffin Books is part of the Penguin Random House group of companies
whose addresses can be found at global.penguinrandomhouse.com.

www.penguin.co.uk   www.puffin.co.uk   www.ladybird.co.uk

Penguin
Random House
UK

First published by David Fickling Books 2002
Published by Picture Corgi 2003
Published in this edition by Puffin Books 2019
001

Printed in China
A CIP catalogue record for this book is available from the British Library

ISBN: 978-0-241-38168-7
All correspondence to:
Puffin Books, Penguin Random House Children's
80 Strand, London WC2R ORL

MIX
Paper from
responsible sources
FSC® C018179

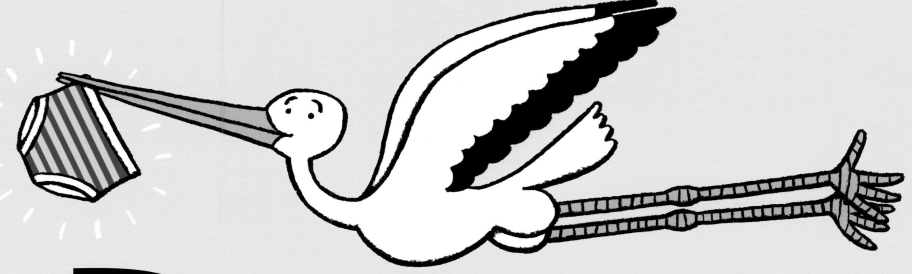

Pants

Giles Andreae
Nick Sharratt

PUFFIN

To P.C. – G.A.

For Lucy – N.S.

Small pants, big pants

Giant frilly pig pants

New pants, blue pants one, two, three

Pants you can wear
if you're **ten feet tall!**

Loose pants, tight pants

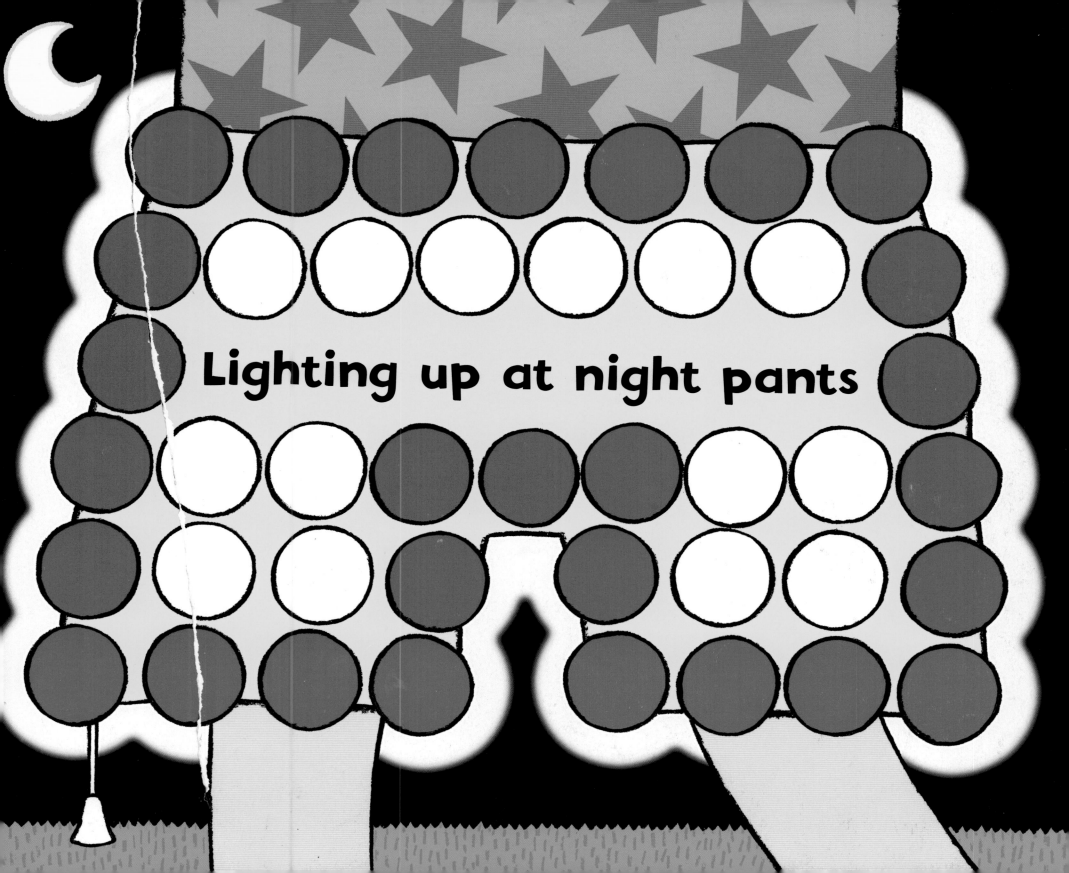

Lighting up at night pants

no pants at all!

Pants on your head when you've gone crazy!

Funny pants,
money pants

Wear them when it's sunny pants

Have you seen these bunny pants?

- yes I have!

Wear them when
You're happy pants

Fairy pants, hairy pants

What a lot of lovely

pants there are!

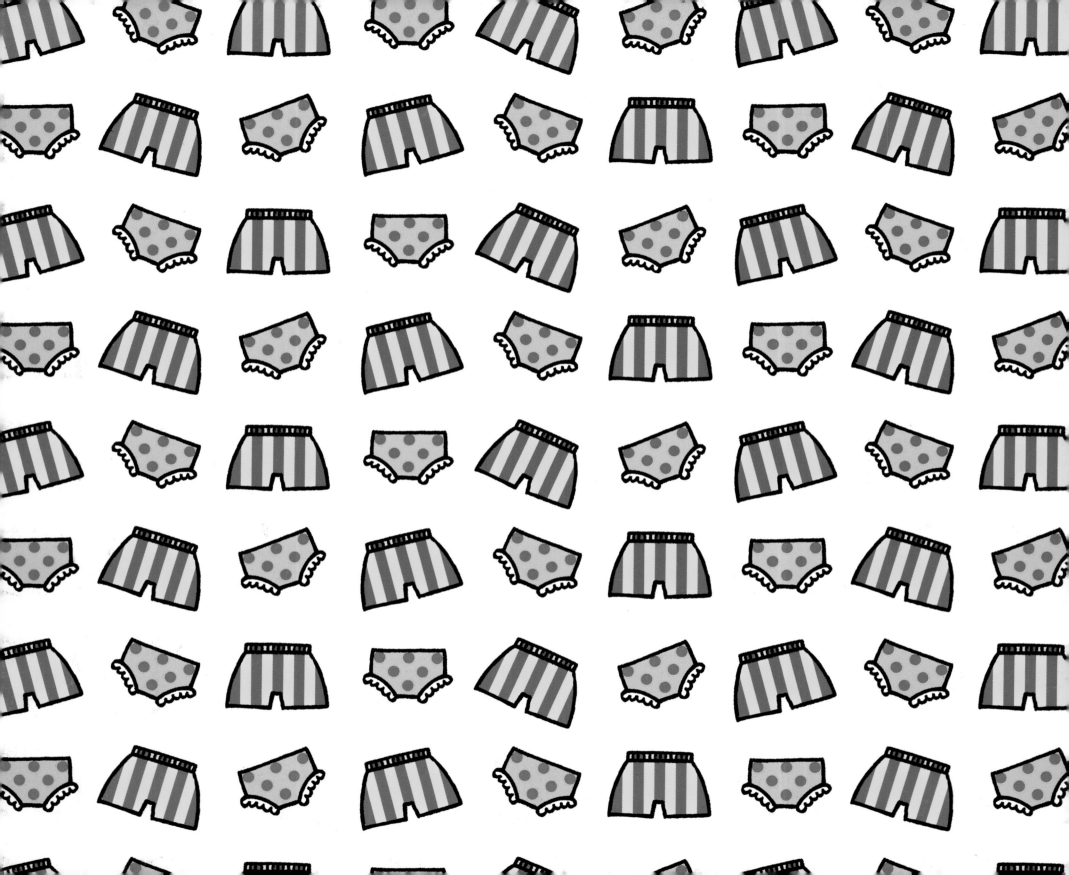

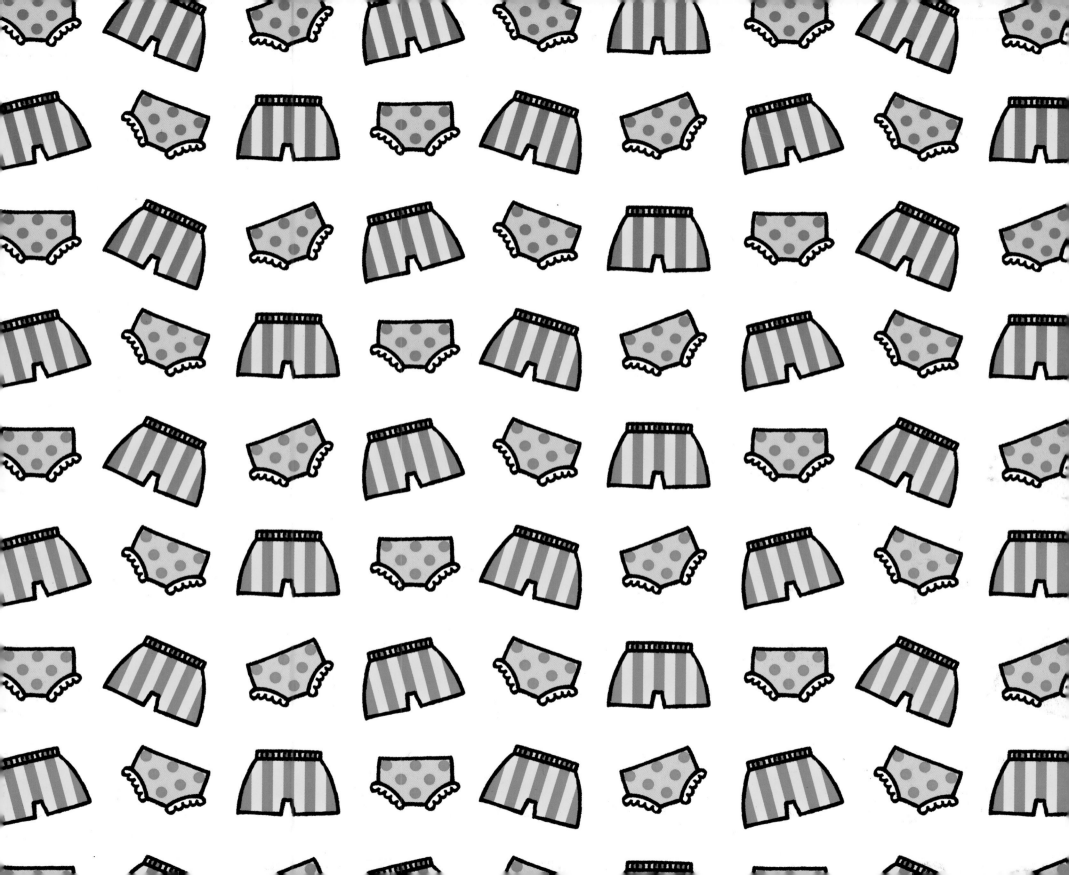

More books written by Giles Andreae

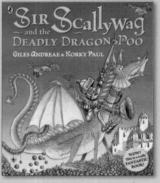

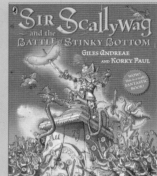

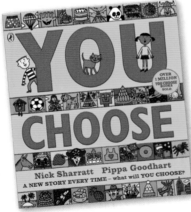

and illustrated by Nick Sharratt